Aliyah and the STEMsational Problem Solvers:

WHAT'S COOKING?

Written by Dr. Chris Goldberg

illustrated by Ryker Cashin and Hope Goldsborough

This book is dedicated to
Max Rappaport, my grandfather and role model,
and Marguerite "Marge" Brown,
my STEM colleague and friend.

Aliyah and STEMsational Problem Solvers: What's Cooking? By Chris Goldberg

Published by STEMsational Problem Solvers LLC

chrisgoldbergbooks.com

Copyright © 2022 by Chris Goldberg

All rights reserved. No portion of this book may be reproduced in any form without permission from the publisher, except as permitted by U.S. copyright law. For permissions contact: stemsationalps@gmail.com

Cover and Illustrations by Ryker Cashin and Hope Goldsborough

Book Interior Designer/Graphic Designer: Gabrielle Tranchitella

Copy Editors: Kristen Imperiale and Jan Spiro

ISBN: 979-8-9870896-0-6

Library of Congress Control Number: 2022919483

Printed in the United States

First Edition

Special Thanks to Book Coach, Esther Hershenhorn.

Inspiration For This Book

Dear Reader,

Believe in Yourself!

My life began on a farm in Dinwiddie County, Virginia. At an early age, I realized that the farm was not the place for me, and I began to dream and think about bigger options.

I knew education was the key to achieving my dream, so I worked hard in high school to get a scholarship to college. After college, I had a dream to work for the government, where I could earn a good salary. It took hard work, commitment, and patience but my dream came true when I was offered a job at the Naval Proving Ground in Dahlgren, VA.

Dream BIG!

Throughout my professional career, I faced some challenges but I always believed that I could overcome. I was honored to work beside brilliant scientists from whom I learned so much. I am proud of my contributions that are used in the GPS today.

Never Give Up!

You, too, can achieve your dreams. Find your passion and find mentors to help build on your passion. Participate in activities that bring your passion to life. Believe in yourself. Make a goal and when you have achieved that goal, set a new one.

Gladys B. West

- Dr. Gladys B. West

Mathematician whose calculations contributed to the development of the modern GPS System

Whiskers! You ruined my plan!
Aliyah

uffin Mix

Recipe

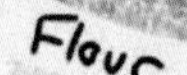
Flour
Brown Sugar

“WHISSSSSKKKKEERSSSSS! Oh, no!”

White and brown sugar, flour, and baking powder covered Aliyah’s kitchen table, with cat paw prints everywhere. Minutes before, the recyclable bags that held the dry ingredients sat inside Aliyah’s school backpack.

“I needed these ingredients, Whiskers,” Aliyah explained, “for my STEMsational project. My team is baking pumpkin muffins at school today!”

Whiskers raised his paw and purred, “Meow.”

“Sorry! No time for excuses. Mom’s left for work, and the bus is almost here.”

Aliyah spent the bus ride to Dr. Gladys West Elementary School picturing the disappointment on the faces of her teammates, Graciela and Drew. The pumpkin muffins they’d planned to bake during cooking class were supposed to win the “Best Dessert Contest” for the National STEM Week Celebration.

“How could we win now if we’re missing four ingredients?” sighed Aliyah.

Flo
Spelling Bee
And here is our annual Spelling Bee champion...
Flo!!!

Hey, I'm a winner too!

“Our team will just need to work hard to find a solution, the way my older sister Flo worked hard to win the spelling bee,” she reasoned. “Flo’s always winning something. I can, too!”

Aliyah squeezed her eyes shut to remember the powerful message on the portrait of her heroine, Dr. Gladys West, hanging in the school’s main hall. Dr. West was one of the first Black mathematicians hired by the United States Navy. She made many vital calculations in creating the GPS, short for Global Positioning System, so people could always find their way.

"But, how can my STEM Team find its way this time?" Aliyah wondered as the bus began to empty. "Unless we use the Engineering Design Process our STEM teacher Dr. Rappo taught us."

In class, Drew and Graciela took one look at Aliyah and knew something was wrong.

"I'm so sorry," Aliyah said, "but Whiskers did it again!"

She held up the torn bags used to hold their recipe's dry ingredients.

"We will need to use our STEM smarts to problem solve and create a solution."

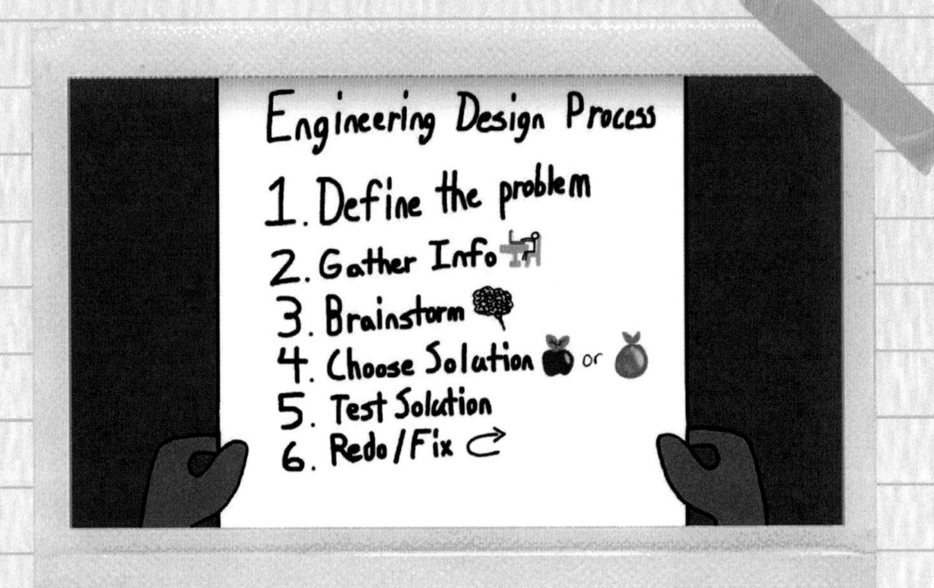

"That's right," Graciela said. "We're a team, right? Besides, we fixed every disaster Whiskers has caused. Remember when he sat on your keyboard and locked you out of your laptop?"

"Or, what about the time he knocked over your robot and caused your computer code to go haywire?" Drew asked.

"You're right!" Aliyah said. "We used Dr. Rappo's Engineering Design Process then to work out solutions. We'll use it again!"

Drew paged through his STEM notebook.

"We'll brainstorm ideas," he said. "Next we'll create and select and then finalize solutions."

"And if we have to," Graciela said, "we'll redo every step. That's what teams do."

Aliyah agreed, but she still worried. They needed Dr. Rappo's problem solving method to work. National STEM Day, held November 8, was their chance to honor Dr. West every year.

Aliyah read everything she could about Dr. Gladys West. When Gladys was young, her parents worked on a farm and didn't have money to send her to college.

But Gladys studied hard and achieved her dreams. She earned a scholarship to college and became a STEM legend and later completed a Ph.D. Aliyah also learned that Gladys loved pumpkin muffins as a child.

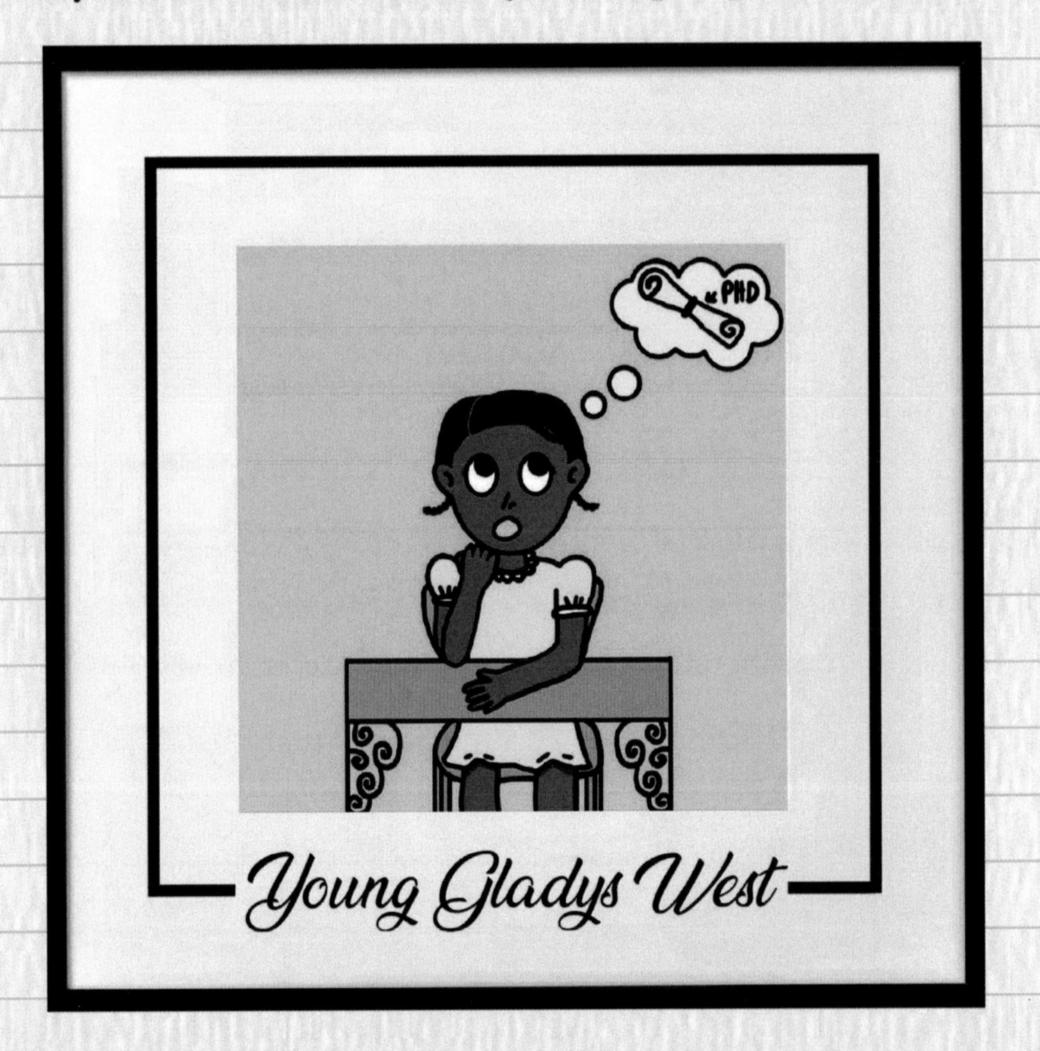

Just last week, Dr. Rappo told Aliyah after class, "You're a STEM natural, just like our school's namesake, Dr. West." Aliyah knew those were words he'd never spoken to Flo.

That night she shared her Big Dream with Whiskers, "Maybe one day, Dr. Rappo will invite my team and me to join his STEMsational Club!"

baking
challenge
dessert
what should we do?

Aliyah couldn't stop worrying as the team entered Mrs. Durkin's cooking classroom.

Graciela dismissed Aliyah's doubts.

"Hope's team is baking pumpkin pie, so typical. Alex's team is baking chocolate chip cookies, so easy. TJ's team is working on a key lime pie, too difficult."

"But, we only have 60 minutes and we're missing four ingredients!" Aliyah reminded her.

Just then, Dr. Rappo stopped by to announce he would be judging each team's dessert.

"What would he think of his STEM natural now?" Aliyah said.

"We've got this," Graciela declared. "Drew will take the notes and I'll oversee the mixing. Remember, my mom is a restaurant chef and I love baking. We'll just need to brainstorm how to find the missing ingredients."

Aliyah's team took to their corner table. The three other teams began gathering pots, bowls, and pans.

"Here's what we have," Graciela announced. She checked off the ingredients on the printed recipe card:

Ingredient List

2 cups of flour ✗
1/2 cup of white sugar ✗
1/2 cup of brown sugar ✗
2 teaspoons of cinnamon ✓
1 teaspoon of baking soda ✗
1/2 teaspoon of salt ✓
1/4 teaspoon of ground cloves ✓
1/4 teaspoon of nutmeg ✓
1- 15 ounce can of pure pumpkin puree ✓
1 teaspoon of vanilla extract ✓

Mrs. Durkin had given each group the eggs they'd need. Aliyah looked at the clock: 50 minutes left. The recipe card shouted out the missing ingredients. Time to problem solve!

“Wait!” Graciela said. “Remember when we helped Alex’s team last week by giving him some of our eggs? We can barter and trade to get what we’re missing.”

Soon, Alex returned the favor by giving the team extra flour, and Hope offered white sugar in return for some of their team’s pureed pumpkin. Once Graciela offered free cooking tips and the team promised everyone a pumpkin muffin, TJ sent over baking soda.

Aliyah looked about the room. Everyone was mixing. She looked at the clock: 40 minutes left, and they were still missing brown sugar!

Just then, Mrs. Silver, the cafeteria lady, stopped by the class to speak with Mrs. Durkin.

"I've got it!" Drew shouted. "I'm always helping Mrs. Silver with the lunchroom computers, and she always tells me to come by for whatever I need. They must have brown sugar."

Drew took off for the cafeteria.

Drew's run only took 6 minutes off the clock and immediately the team began mixing the muffin ingredients.

Meanwhile, the other teams were working hard. Hope was pouring the batter into the pie shell. Alex was scooping cookies onto the baking sheets. TJ and his team were still squeezing the limes.

Mrs. Durkin's classroom smelled of chocolate and pumpkins. Aliyah looked at the clock: 25 minutes left. Just enough time to pour the muffin batter into the paper muffin cups that fit inside the tins. The muffins needed only 20 minutes baking time.

"Oh, no!" Aliyah cried,"Guess who left the muffin cups at home? Me!"

Aliyah couldn't let Flo be the only one in the family to shine. Her team was determined to win. She repeated to herself, "Never give up!"

Graciela and Drew began brainstorming again. Maybe another team had extra liners? Maybe Drew could cut muffin shells from his notebook pages?

Graciela came up with the winning idea: "We don't need paper. We can use Mrs. Durkin's olive oil."

Aliyah looked at the clock. Only 23 minutes left. Enough time to gently spray the insides of the baking tins with olive oil, fill them with batter, and get them inside the oven.

Dr. Rappo arrived to check on the teams and judge the contest. He approached Aliyah's team.

"How is the process going?" he asked.

"We found our way," Aliyah said. "Thanks to your lessons on the Engineering Design Process."

"And teamwork," Graciela said.

Drew added: "Let's hear it for Dr. Rappo's favorite word, 'Collaboration.'"

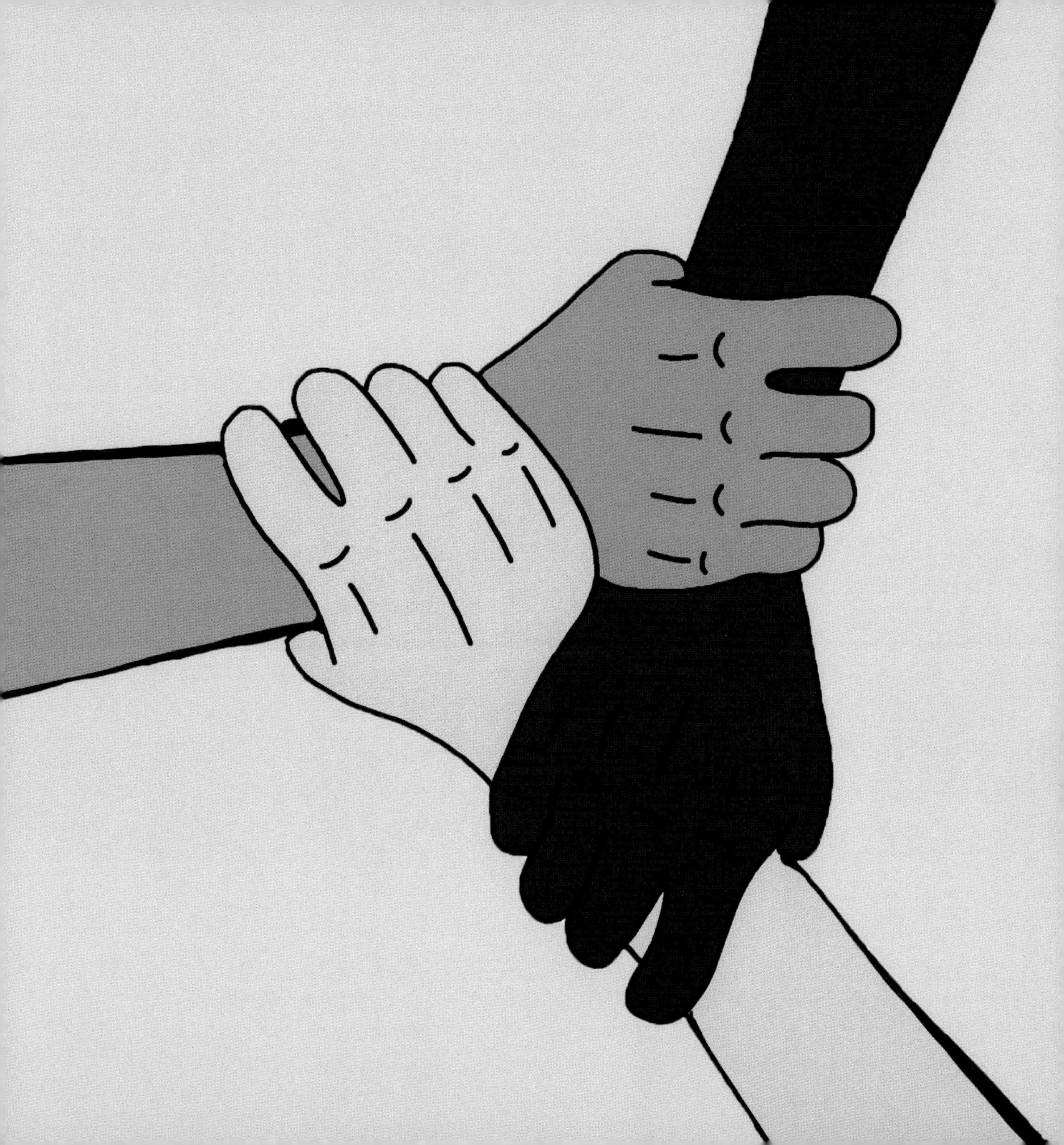

1 print
2 game.
StartButton(
3 wait(
4 unt
TIME'S U

Had their STEM team won the Best Dessert Contest? That was the question. The answer came soon enough.

"All four STEM teams should be proud of their sweet victories," Dr. Rappo announced. "Congratulations to Hope and her team's pumpkin pie, winners of the Best Dessert Contest."

Aliyah's team was heartbroken.

"We worked so hard," Graciela whispered.

"We did, and we overcame so much," Aliyah whispered back.

Aliyah congratulated Hope's team, but she couldn't hide her disappointment.

Fortunately, Dr. Rappo hadn't finished his announcements.

"I've decided to invite one 4th grade STEM team to join the 5th and 6th graders in our STEMsational Club."

Aliyah crossed her fingers. Graciela crossed her ankles. Drew crossed his arms behind his back.

"I am inviting Aliyah, Drew, and Graciela to join our STEMsational Club," said Dr. Rappo. "They have demonstrated Dr. West's true team spirit."

Aliyah high-fived Drew and Graciela and said proudly, "We're winners after all."

On some school days, when no one was looking, Aliyah would stop by Dr. West's portrait to share the day's news before boarding the school bus. Today was one of those days.

"Thank you, Dr. West," Aliyah whispered, "I know my dream was BIG, but I never gave up. I can't wait to tell Flo we were invited to join Dr. Rappo's STEM Club. I can also tell Whiskers he's off the hook."

Aliyah knew if Dr. West could, she would have winked.

Dr. Gladys B. West

Dr. Gladys B. West is a mathematician who, after many years, was recognized for being a leader of teams that completed the model, or computations, responsible for creating the Global Positioning System (GPS.)

At the age of 87, she was inducted into the Air Force Space and Missile Pioneers Hall of Fame during a ceremony at the Pentagon.

Dr. West worked at the U.S. Naval Proving Grounds in Dahlgren,

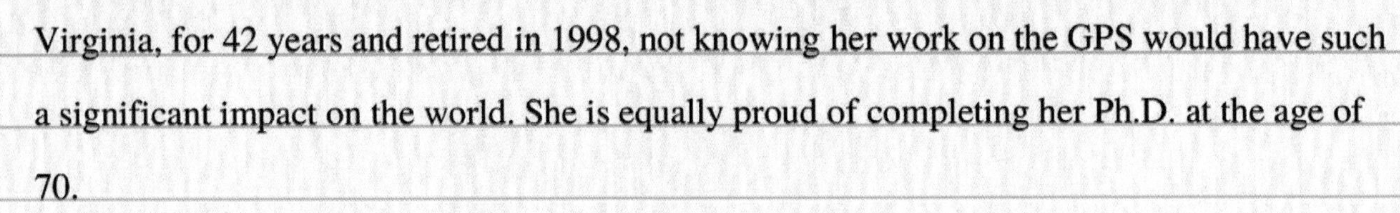

Virginia, for 42 years and retired in 1998, not knowing her work on the GPS would have such a significant impact on the world. She is equally proud of completing her Ph.D. at the age of 70.

Dr. West advocates for women and minorities in STEM to students of all ages. You can learn even more about her life and work by reading her autobiography, *It Began With a Dream.*

About STEM

STEM is an acronym for the fields of science, technology, engineering, and mathematics. Evidence shows that emphasizing STEM across the curriculum can assist in student achievement through collaboration, critical thinking, creativity, curiosity, decision making, leadership, entrepreneurship, and other skills.

Discussion of STEM-related programs has become a national priority due to a shortage of college students pursuing degrees in STEM-related fields, especially among women and minorities and students with disabilities. It is predicted that the number of STEM jobs in future years will rise at a high rate as the nation seeks greater solutions to problems that impact people of all ages.

Some of the most popular STEM jobs include positions in programming, engineering, medicine, robotics, aerospace, data analysis, and many others. It is important for parents, educators, and leaders to support STEM programs and provide access for all students.

About the Author

Dr. Chris Goldberg spent 27 years as a Special Education, Computer, and STEM Teacher /Coach in suburban Philadelphia public schools. Chris received his Doctor of Education in Special Education in 2005 from Arcadia University and was honored as a Philadelphia Eagles/Axalta All-Pro STEM Teacher in 2019. He has dedicated himself to teaching and advocating for underserved students of all backgrounds. He currently works for Temple University as a Student Teacher Field Supervisor in Special Education and coaches student teachers in the Philadelphia School District and surrounding suburbs.

About the Illustrators

Ryker Cashin is a 10-year-old student in the 5th Grade at Norwood School. He loves to animate and draw. He was inspired to draw when he saw artists making people happy. Ryker loves games, drawing, building, and his dog Poppy. He wants to pursue a master's degree and work in the field of animation. Ryker believes that "anything that can be dreamed can be done with the power of teamwork and dedication."

Hope Goldsborough is also a 10-year-old student in the 5th Grade at Norwood School. Hope loves all things that are related to STEM. She also loves and adores her 2-year-old cat, Nimbus. She enjoys reading, drawing, theater, gaming, watching anime, playing the flute, and being on the softball team. Love for illustrating runs in the family since her Pop-Pop and Grandpop are talented in drawing as well. She is inspired by strong female role models like Gladys B. West. One thing that Hope would say to the world is, "Love yourself. Don't let other people tell you who you are and who you need to be."

The Engineering Design Process

The Engineering Design Process (EDP) is a series of steps engineers use to solve problems. It is used in STEM education to teach students of all ages a problem-solving method to use in all classes. The EDP is best used in a team setting where collaboration can be fostered.

Some of the most common steps in the EDP in the classroom include:

- Identify the Problem
- Understand/Research the Problem
- Brainstorm for Possible Solutions
- Develop Solutions
- Select the Best Solution
- Build or Draw the Solution or Prototype
- Test and Evaluate the Solution or Prototype
- Communicate or Present Results
- Improve or Redesign the Solution or Prototype as Needed

This process can have more or fewer steps. It should always be done in a team, and when done in school, with enough supervision to foster creative ideas, higher-order learning, and more advanced solutions.

Stem Resources

STEM Careers Coalition™ – *https://stemcareerscoalition.org*

Connects STEM careers with young learners.

NASA STEM Engagement - *https://nasa.gov/stem/foreducators/k-12*

Teachers can search all resources to find specific lesson plans, videos, publications, and websites to enhance traditional science lessons, such as Earth science, life science, physical science, and space.

Women in STEM - *https://womeninstem.org/*

Empowers and encourages high school girls to be a part of the movement to increase female representation in STEM.

National Science Foundation - *https://NSF.org*

Provides the latest news in science, including current research.

Official STEM Website - *https://STEM.org*

Launched in 2001, STEM.org is the longest continually-operating, privately-held STEM education research and credentialing organization in America.

Smithsonian Girls and Women in STEM - *https://ssec.si.edu/girls-and-women-in-stem*

Lists STEM resources for all students, girls and boys.

Library of Congress Historical Women in STEM - *https://blogs.loc.gov/headlinesandheroes/2022/03/historical-women-in-stem/*

Listing of many highly impactful women in STEM.

STEM For All Foundation - *http://stemforallfoundation.com/*

Provides access and equitable STEM opportunities for all students.

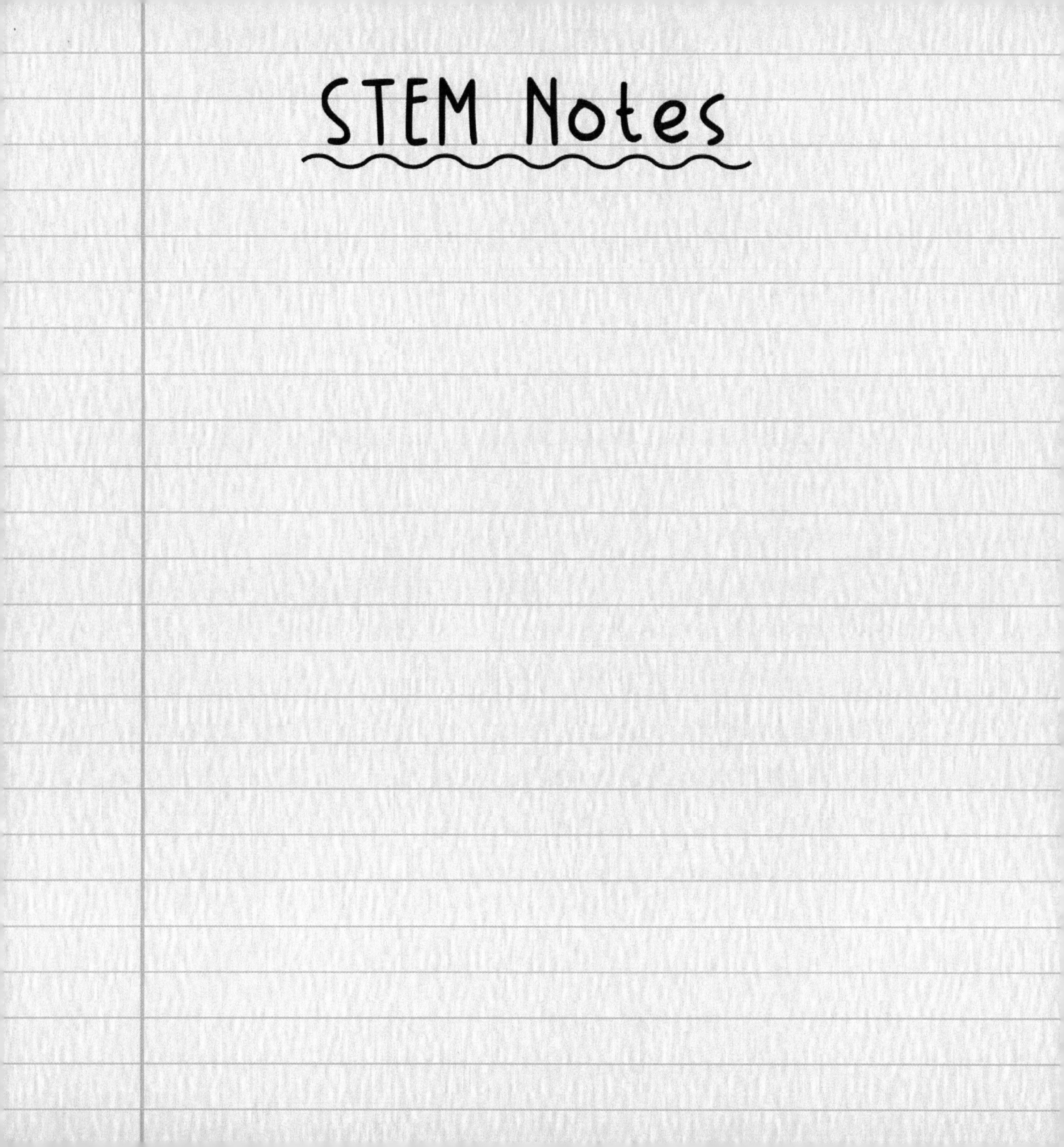
STEM Notes

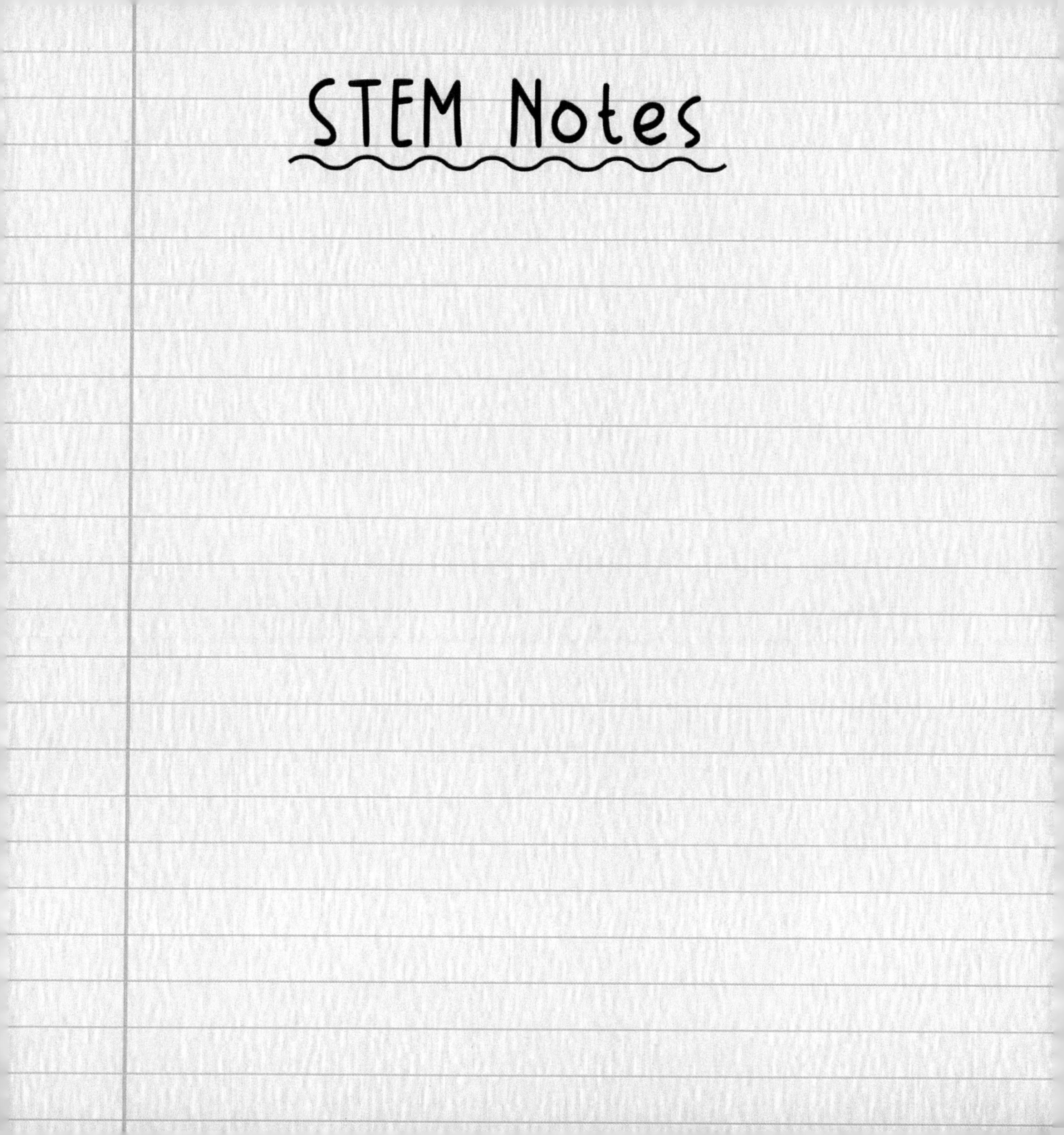
STEM Notes

Made in the USA
Middletown, DE
28 November 2022